Saturday Popular Concerts.

———

DIRECTOR—Mr. S. ARTHUR CHAPPELL.

Four Hundred and Eighty-ninth Concert.*

PROGRAMME FROM THE WORKS OF

Various Masters.

———

SATURDAY AFTERNOON, NOVEMBER 21st, 1874.

———

Fourth Concert of the Seventeenth Season.

QUINTET, in A minor, Op. 107, for Pianoforte, two Violins, Viola, and Violoncello. *Joachim Raff.*

(First performance at the Popular Concerts.)

Allegro mosso assai—A minor.
Allegro vivace quasi presto—C sharp minor; with
alternativo—A major.
Andante quasi larghetto mosso—F major.
Allegro brioso patetico—A minor.

Dr. HANS VON BÜLOW, Herr STRAUS,

Herr L. RIES, Mr. ZERBINI, and Signor PIATTI.

Allegro mosso assai (leading theme).

(Second theme.)

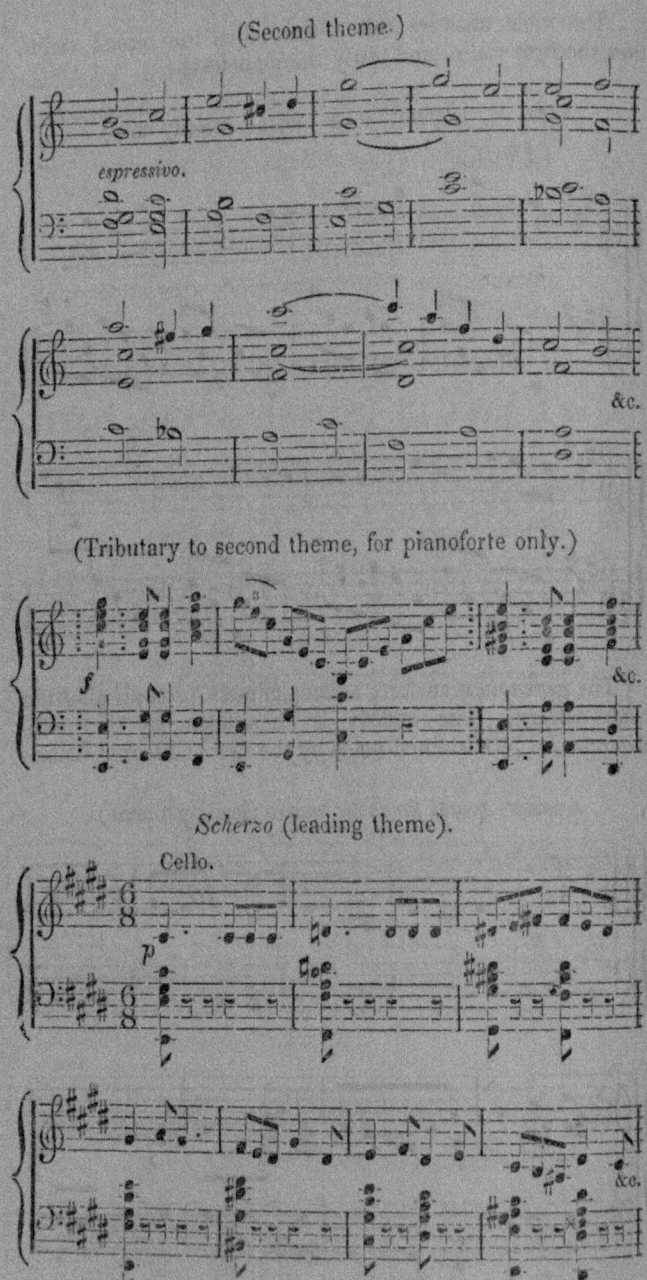

espressivo.

&c.

(Tributary to second theme, for pianoforte only.)

&c.

Scherzo (leading theme).

Cello.

&c.

The viola answers this theme, then the second violin, then the first violin, and lastly the pianoforte.

Trio, or Alternativo (A major—melody only).

1st Violin.

The *arpeggio* pianoforte accompaniment proceeds after the same pattern. The melody is then taken by the viola, accompanied in sustained notes by the first and second violins.

Andante quasi larghetto mosso (leading theme).

&c.

(Second theme—tonic minor.)

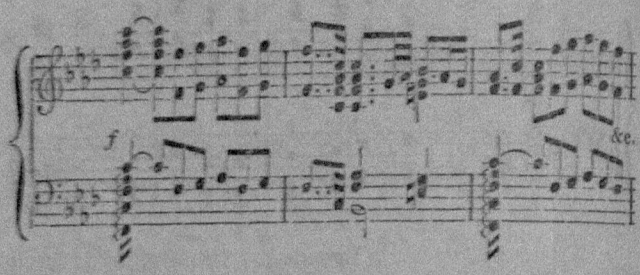

Finale, allegro brioso patetico (leading theme—melody only).

2nd Violin and Cello in octaves.

1st Violin.

(Tributary.)

(Episode.)

(From the Crystal Palace analytical programme—
Nov. 14, 1874.)

Herr Joachim Raff—next to Wagner himself, the most prominent orchestral writer in the band which ranges itself under the banner of that daring and powerful chief—was born at Lachen, in Switzerland, on the 27th May, 1822. He began life as a schoolmaster, though he appears always to have practised music. Struggling on with the true perseverance of a genuine artist, in the latter part of 1843 he

was most favourably introduced by Mendelssohn to Messrs.
Breitkopf and Härtel, the well-known publishers of Leipsic,
all the more favourably because the motive of the act arose
from no personal knowledge, but from the impression which
his compositions had made on that great and genial master.
We are fortunately in a position to give a copy of the letter,
which, besides its testimony to Mendelssohn's anxiety to
serve a rising musician, shows how voluminously Raff was
already writing even at that early date :—

"Leipsic, 20th November, 1843.

"Most respected Sirs,

"I have received the enclosed letter and compositions,
and cannot refrain from submitting them to you in the hope that
you may be able to indulge both the writer and myself with a
favourable answer to our wish. Were the pieces only signed by
some well-known name, I am persuaded they would have a very
large sale, for the contents are such that it would be difficult to
believe that many of the pieces were not by Liszt, Döhler, and
other eminent players. The composition is elegant and faultless
throughout, and in the most modern style; but now comes the fact
that no one knows the name of the composer, which entirely alters
the case. Perhaps a single piece might be taken out of each set, or
possibly you may find that one or two of those for which I per-
sonally care least (*e.g.* the Galops) are more suited for the public
taste; in a word, perhaps you may somehow be induced to print
something out of the collection. If my hearty recommendation
will have any weight, I most willingly add it to the request of my
young friend. In any case, I must ask you to try the pieces over,
and refer them to those friends who usually advise you in such
cases, and then let me know the result, returning the letter at the
same time, but I trust with only a little of the music. Such is my
hope, which I beg you to pardon and excuse.

"Yours faithfully,

"F. M. B."

In 1846 Raff made Mendelssohn's personal acquaintance
at Cologne, and was urged by him to complete his musical
studies at Leipsic, but the scheme was frustrated by Mendelssohn's death in 1847. After a short residence in Cologne,
Raff went to Stuttgart, where he made the acquaintance of
Herr von Bülow. Here he resided for some time, composing
much music, but finding it impossible to get any of it per-
formed; and a curious anecdote is told of Lindpaintner, the
chief conductor of the Orchestra, which shows how much
greater was his care for his own reputation than his desire to
assist a rising brother artist. In 1849 Raff changed his
abode to Weimar, and then to Wiesbaden, where he has
since permanently lived. His industry is something extraordinary, considering the late period at which he began his
career, and the size and careful finish of many of his works.

If the present is a fair specimen of his orchestral works, then they are certainly remarkable, whether belonging to the very highest class or not. On the writer the Symphony makes a similar impression to that made by Victor Hugo's poetry. There is the same originality in both, the same exuberance, the same force and picturesqueness, the same love of effect, and also, it must be admitted, the same tendency to exaggeration, and the same occasional want of refinement, not to use a harsher word.

Herr Raff's published instrumental works comprise six* symphonies, a sinfonietta, a suite, five overtures, and a march; two compositions for pianoforte and orchestra, five string quartets, a quintet for piano and strings, four trios for ditto, and five sonatas for piano and violin. In addition, the list contains operas and other large vocal compositions, and a host of smaller pieces, numbering in all not far short of two hundred. The "interest in something new and untried," and the pleasure "in that kind of uncertainty which leaves room for the musician and the public to have an opinion"—which Mendelssohn felt so keenly, and expressed so strongly, in one of his letters to Hiller, attaches itself in a peculiar degree to Raff's music. Much as it is played in Germany, in England it is all but unknown. A chamber-piece or two, and a couple of movements from an orchestral piece, are all that the great musical public of England knows of a composer whose works already amount to the large number already mentioned, and whose name is found in almost every concert programme in his native country.

("G.")

---

* No. 1, "Vaterland Sinfonie" in D (obtained the prize at Vienna in 1862). No. 2, in C. No. 3, in G minor. No. 4, "Wald-Sinfonie," in F. No. 5, "Lenore," in E. No. 6, in D minor.

—

SONG, Mlle. NITA GAETANO.

(Azor and Zemira.)   *Spohr.*

Rose, softly blooming, form'd to allure,
Emblem of nature, simple, and pure;
Storms press around thee;
Yet, gentle flower,
Smiles still are thine,
The charm of the bower!

Nurtur'd of Heaven! thy beauties I'll wear;
Pride of my bosom! I'll cherish thee there;
Smiles still are thine
In decay's wasting hour;
So, gentle flow'r,
Peacefully smiling, oh! let me be,
Living and dying, sweet Rose, like thee!

From the opera of *Zemire und Azor*, an English version
of which,* some forty years ago, was produced with eminent success at Covent Garden Theatre, under the manage-
ment of Mr. Charles Kemble. *Zemire und Azor* was
composed by Spohr in the year 1817, and brought out at
Frankfort-on-the-Maine just after his return from a tour in
Italy, where, through his admirable performances on the
violin, he was proclaimed by many, even among the Italians
themselves, the rival of Paganini. This opera, combined with
the Symphony in D minor (No. 2), first gave rise to that
unbounded enthusiasm which the works of Spohr excited
among musicians in this country, an enthusiasm which even
now is hardly quelled, and which, whatever prejudicial in-
fluence it may have indirectly exercised, did much to awaken
the long-dormant instinct of our young composers for something artistically far superior to anything that had previously
been esteemed among them.

---

* Under the title of *Azor and Zemira* (the *Beauty and the Beast*)
—Miss Inverarity, Misses Mary and Harriet Cawse taking the
principal female characters.

SUITE DE PIÈCES, in F major (*Suites Anglaises*, No. 4), for Pianoforte alone.   *J. S. Bach.*

(Second performance at the Popular Concerts.)

1. Prelude—allegro moderato.
2. Allemande – allegro moderato.
3. Courante—molto allegro.
4. Sarabande—andante sostenuto.
5. Minuets—Nos. 1 and 2—andante con moto.
6. Gigue—presto.

Dr. HANS VON BÜLOW.

Prelude (leading theme).

(Tributary.)

(Return to theme, on dominant pedal.)

Theme.

&c.

Allemande.

Courante.

Sarabande.

andante sostenuto.

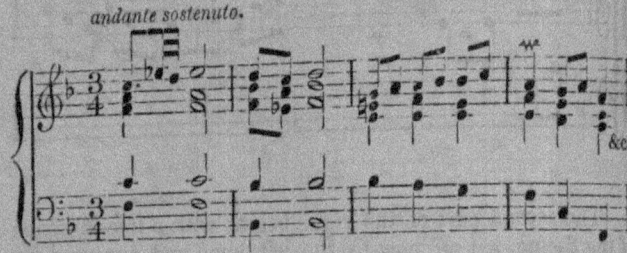

&c.

Minuet, No. 1.

andante con moto.

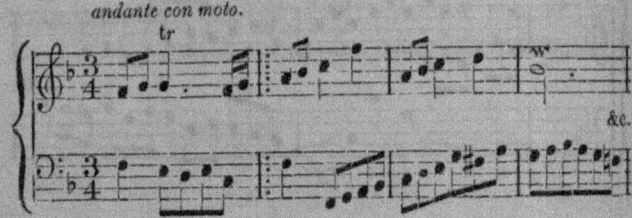

&c.

Minuet, No. 2 (relative minor).

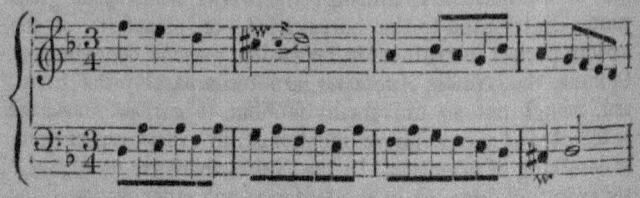

Gigue.

presto.

The second part of the *gigue* begins with a free inversion of the theme, led off now by the left hand and answered by the right, as in the first section the right was answered by the left :—

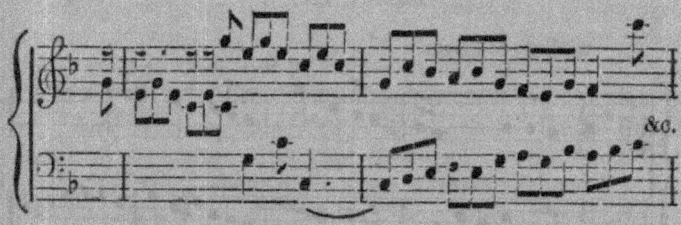

Next to the well-known *Clavier bien temperé* (48 Preludes and Fugues in all the keys), the *Suites de Pièces* of John Sebastian Bach occupy the highest place in the estimation of connoisseurs, amongst the works which that great master contributed to the harpsichord—or pianoforte, as the modern perfect instrument is, for evident reasons, denominated. Of these, the *Suites Anglaises* are incomparably the finest, and, though not so universally familiar to earnest musicians as the *chef-d'œuvre* above mentioned, in every respect quite as deserving of attention. In the *Suites* there are no fugues,* nor even fughettas, as in the fantasias and other works of the kind which Bach produced with such inexhaustible fertility. A *suite* consists of a chain of movements, generally all in the same key, which, as the whole occupies a very considerable time in performance, renders it advisable sometimes, for the sake of avoiding monotony, to omit one, and occasionally even

---

* Five out of the grand *Suites de Pièces* composed by Handel for Queen Caroline, or the Princess Anne—when very little was known of Bach's harpsichord music in Germany, much less in England— contain fugues more or less elaborate.

more. It will be observed, that, in almost every instance, Bach* begins the *suite* with an *allegro* of large proportions, in which is plainly suggested the form of the symphonic first movement, the development, if not absolute invention, of which has been solely attributed to Haydn. Let any one examine the *allegro* in G minor, that in D minor, and that in F major (introduced to-day), belonging to the *Suites Anglaises*, and he will hardly fail to remark that Bach, in a very great measure, anticipated Haydn in the most important of all discoveries connected with the art of musical composition. Independently of this interesting fact, however, the *Suites de Pièces* are entitled to the highest admiration, on account of their intrinsic beauty; added to which, as studies for the attainment of fluent, even, and vigorous execution, they are invaluable. Pianists who are able to perform them with correctness and facility need expend very little labour in conquering the difficulties presented by the works of more recent composers. It was by the constant practice of Bach's music that Clementi, Dussek, and John Cramer, obtained that command of "*legato*" for which they were unrivalled; and this, while among the rarest of mechanical endowments, is precisely the one most indispensable to the acquisition of a graceful and expressive style.

The Suite in F major was first introduced by Madame Arabella Goddard, at the sixth concert of the second season—Dec. 19, 1859.

---

* Unlike Handel, with whom this rule becomes an exception almost as rare.

** Dr. HANS VON BÜLOW will perform on one of Messrs. JOHN BROADWOOD and SONS' Concert Grand Pianofortes.

PERSIAN LOVE SONG. *Rubinstein.*

Mlle. NITA GAETANO.

"OH! COULD IT REMAIN SO FOR EVER!"

Swift roll at my feet amber waves of the Koor,
　Brightly dancing in playful endeavour;
Glad smileth the sun, my heart floweth o'er,
　Oh! could it remain so for ever!

Darkness draweth nigh, clouds are veiling the light,
　From the star of my love must I sever;
In deepest midnight my heart burneth bright,
　Oh! could it remain so for ever!

In th' unfathom'd depth of thy dark starry eyes
　Glows the tide of my love, staying never;
Come, my fair, dissolve me in sighs,
　Oh! could it remain so for ever!

QUARTET, in F major, Op. 59, No. 1, for two Violins, Viola, and Violoncello. *Beethoven.*

(Tenth performance at the Popular Concerts.)

Allegro—F major.
Allegretto vivace sempre scherzando—B flat major.
Adagio molto e mesto—F minor; leading to
Theme Russe, Allegro and Presto—F major.

Herr STRAUS, Herr L. RIES, Mr. ZERBINI, and Signor PIATTI.

The seventh of the seventeen quartets composed by Beethoven, and No. 1 of a set of three, Op. 59, dedicated to Count Rasoumowski, the Russian Ambassador at Vienna, and a great musical amateur. These Quartets were composed in 1806, about a year after *Fidelio,* and first played (from manuscript copies) in 1807, at Vienna. It was the violoncello part of the Quartet in F major (No. 1) which the celebrated Bernhard Romberg threw on the ground, stamped upon, and declared "unplayable."* It is worth noting that the first movement of the Quartet in F is the earliest among the works

---

* This occurred (or rather is said to have occurred) at the house of Marshall Count Soltykoff, in Moscow, at the commencement of 1812.

of Beethoven in which the opening section is not repeated—
a circumstance for which its unusual length may account.
Mendelssohn used to say that the Rasoumowski Quartet in F
major, and the Quartet No. 11, in F minor, were the most
" thoroughly Beethovenish " of all Beethoven's works.   It was
probably as a compliment to Count Rasoumowski, who had
presented him with the themes, that Beethoven took a Russian
melody for the subject of the *finale* in the first of the Quartets
Op 59 (F major), and another for the *trio* of the *allegretto*
(third movement), in the second (E minor).

Allegro.

(Episode.)

(Principal second theme.)

&c.

(Tributary to second theme.)

Out of the foregoing materials this very originally constructed, lengthily developed, and altogether extraordinary movement is principally constructed. Other episodes might be cited; but to an attentive listener they are unnecessary. There is one, however, of great importance, occurring in the middle part of the movement, to which a few bars will suffice to call attention:—

(Episode.)

(Coda.)

Allegro vivace e sempre scherzando.

2nd Violin.

Violoncello. *p*

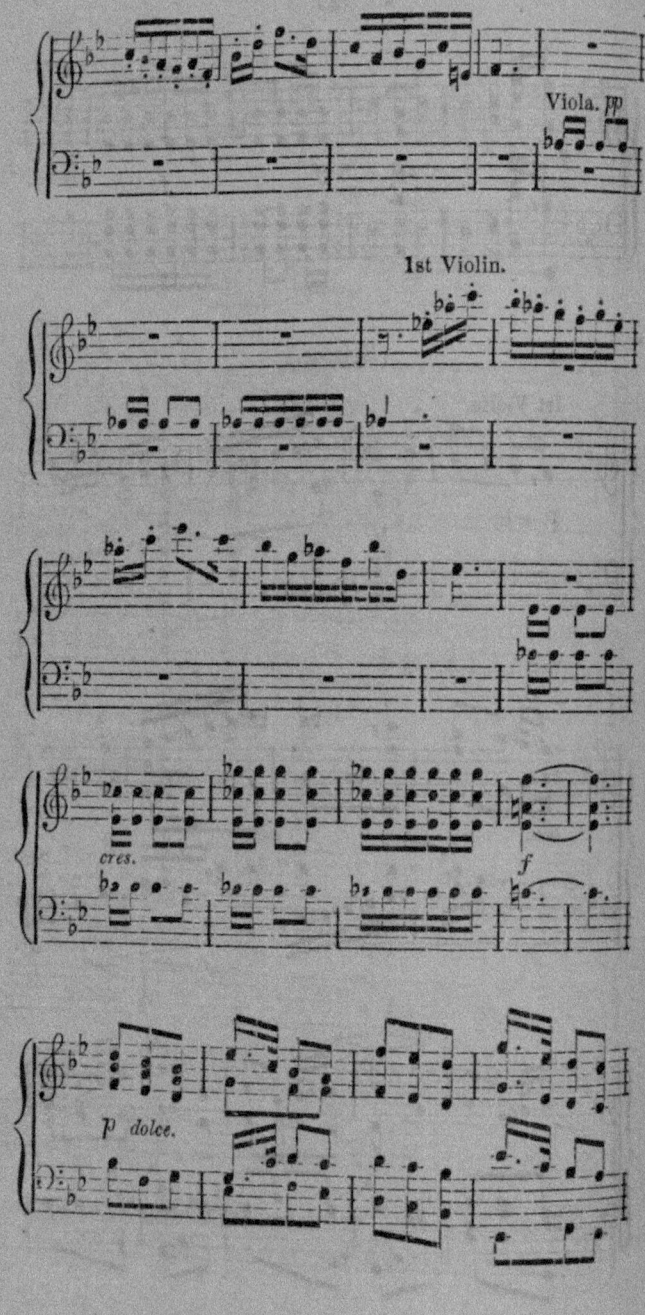

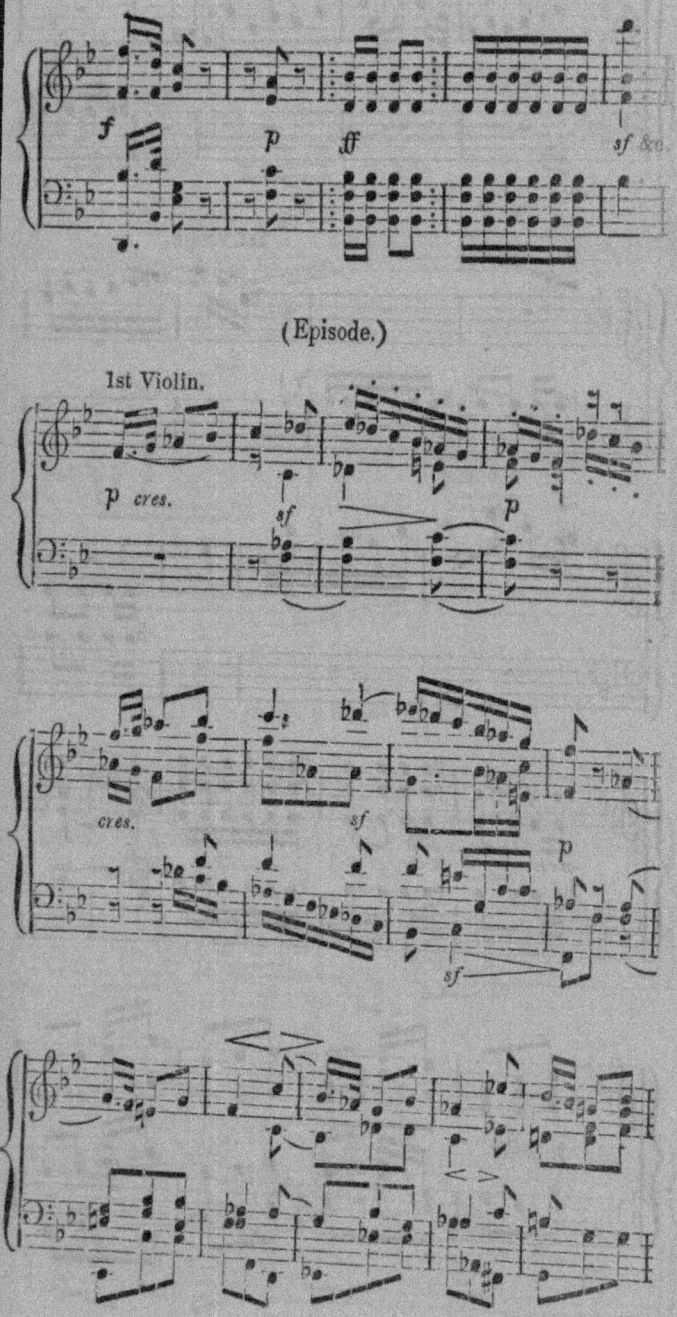

(Episode.)

1st Violin.

Adagio molto e mesto.

(Episode in A flat major.)

Finale, allegro.

&c.

1st Violin.

Russian melody.

Violoncello.

Z

The remainder of this *finale* will speak for itself, without further quotation.

(Coda)

The Quartet in F, Op. 59, No. 1, was first introduced by M. Wieniawski, Herr Ries, Herr Schreurs, and Signor Piatti, at the fourth concert of the first season—March 7, 1859.

END OF THE FOUR HUNDRED AND EIGHTY-NINTH CONCERT.

J. MALLETT, PRINTER, 59, WARDOUR STREET, SOHO. W.

MONDAY POPULAR CONCERTS.

MONDAY EVENING, NOVEMBER 23rd, 1874.

PROGRAMME.

PART I.

QUARTET, in E flat, Op. 71, No. 3, for two Violins, Viola,
and Violoncello .... *Haydn.*

Madame NORMAN-NÉRUDA,

MM. L. RIES, ZERBINI, and PIATTI.

AIR, " Pietà, Signore." .... *Stradella.*

Mr. SANTLEY.

SONATA, in E major, Op. 6, for Pianoforte alone .... *Mendelssohn.*

Miss AGNES ZIMMERMANN.

PART II.

TRIO, in F major, Op. 80, for Pianoforte, Violin, and
Violoncello .... *Schumann.*

Miss AGNES ZIMMERMANN, Madame NORMAN-NÉRUDA,

and Signor PIATTI.

SONG, "The Erl King." .... *Schubert.*

Mr. SANTLEY.

RONDEAU BRILLANT, in B minor, Op. 70, for Pianoforte
and Violin .... *Schubert.*

Miss AGNES ZIMMERMANN and Mme. NORMAN-NÉRUDA.

Conductor - - Sir JULIUS BENEDICT.

2 A